THIS LITTLE TIGER BOOK BELONGS TO:

_____

_____

_____

_____

For Flora, Ron and Elaine
~J.S.

For Glen P.
~T.W.

LITTLE TIGER PRESS
An imprint of Magi Publications
22 Manchester Street, London W1M 5PG
This paperback edition published 1996
First published in Great Britain 1996
Text © 1996 Julie Sykes
Illustrations © 1996 Tim Warnes
Julie Sykes and Tim Warnes have asserted their rights
to be identified as the author and illustrator of this work
under the Copyright, Designs and Patents Act, 1988.
Printed in Belgium by Proost NV, Turnhout
All rights reserved
ISBN 1 85430 289 2
9 11 13 15 17 19 20 18 16 14 12 10 8

I don't want to go to bed!

by Julie Sykes

illustrated by Tim Warnes

Little Tiger Press

Little Tiger was very naughty.
He did not like going to bed.
Every night when Mummy Tiger said,
"Bedtime!"
Little Tiger would say,
"But I don't *want* to go to bed!"

Little Tiger wouldn't let Mummy Tiger clean his face
and paws, and he wouldn't listen to his bedtime story.
One night Mummy Tiger lost her temper.
When Little Tiger said, "I don't want to go to bed!"
Mummy Tiger roared,
"ALL RIGHT, YOU CAN STAY UP ALL NIGHT THEN!"

Little Tiger couldn't believe his good luck.
He scampered off into the jungle before
Mummy Tiger could change her mind.

Little Tiger went to visit his
best friend, Little Lion.
When he arrived,
Little Lion was having
his ears washed.

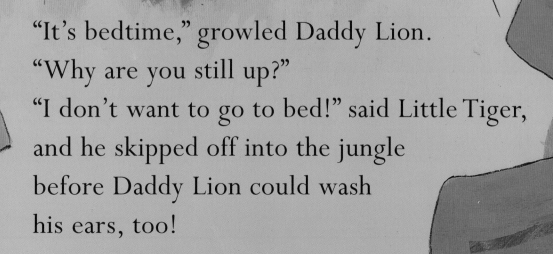

"It's bedtime," growled Daddy Lion.
"Why are you still up?"
"I don't want to go to bed!" said Little Tiger,
and he skipped off into the jungle
before Daddy Lion could wash
his ears, too!

Little Tiger decided to visit his second best friend,
Little Hippo.
He found him splashing in the river,
having a bedtime bath.

"It's bedtime," bellowed Daddy Hippo.
"Why are you still up?"
"I don't want to go to bed!" said Little Tiger,
and he scurried off into the jungle before
Daddy Hippo could give him a bath, too!

Little Elephant was Little Tiger's third best friend.

He went to visit him next.

Little Elephant was not out playing.

He was in bed, listening to his bedtime story.

"It's bedtime," trumpeted Mummy Elephant.

"Why are you still up?"

"I don't want to go to bed!" said Little Tiger,

and he bounced off into the jungle before

Mummy Elephant could put him to bed, too!

Little Tiger thought he
would go and find
Little Monkey,
his fourth best friend.
But he found Mummy
Monkey first. She put
a finger to her lips and
whispered, "Little
Monkey is fast asleep.
Why are you still up?"

"I don't want to go to bed!"
Little Tiger whispered back.
Quickly he tiptoed into the
jungle before Mummy Monkey
made him fall asleep, too!

Little Tiger didn't know where to go next. It was the
first time he had been on his own in the jungle so late.
Even the sun had gone to bed!
Suddenly it seemed very dark.
What was that?

Little Tiger looked up
and saw . . .

. . . two very large yellow eyes
staring back at him!

The eyes belonged to a bush baby.
"Shouldn't you be in bed?" she asked.
"I don't want to go to bed,"
said Little Tiger
bravely. "*You* haven't!"
"That's because I go to
bed when the sun rises,"
said Bush Baby.

"Fancy going to bed in the lovely sunshine!" thought Little Tiger. He shivered and thought how cold and dark it was in the jungle at night.

"I'm going to take you home," said Bush Baby.
"Your mummy and daddy will be worried about you."
"I don't want to go home! I don't want to go to bed!"
said Little Tiger. But he didn't want to be left alone
in the dark either.

So Little Tiger followed Bush Baby through the jungle.
He was glad of her big bright eyes to show him the way
back home.
"We're nearly there," said Bush Baby, as Little Tiger's
steps became slower and slower.

"I don't want to go to . . ." said Little Tiger sleepily,
dragging his paws.

"Ah, there you are," said Mummy Tiger.

"Just in time for bed!"

"I don't want to . . ." yawned Little Tiger,
and he fell fast asleep!
Mummy Tiger tucked him up
and then turned to Bush Baby . . .

. . . but the den was empty.
Bush Baby had disappeared into
the jungle before Mummy Tiger
could tuck *her* up, too!

Join the LITTLE TIGER CLUB
now for lots more
books to enjoy!

Schools can
join too and will
receive a special
enrolment pack.

Join the LITTLE TIGER CLUB now and receive a special Little Tiger goody bag containing badges, pencils and more! Once you become a member you will receive details of special offers, competitions and news of new books. Why not write a book review?
The best reviews received will be published on book covers or in the Little Tiger catalogue.

The LITTLE TIGER CLUB is free to join. Members can cancel their membership at
any time, and are under no obligation to purchase any books.
If you would like details of the Little Tiger Club or a catalogue
of books please contact: Little Tiger Press, 22 Manchester Street,
London W1M 5PG, UK. Telephone 0171 486 0925
Visit our website at: www.littletiger.okukbooks.com